First published in the United States, Great Britain, Canada, Australia, and New Zealand in 2012
by NorthSouth Books Inc., an imprint of NordSüd Verlag AG, CH-8005 Zürich, Switzerland.

Translated by Rebecca K. Morrison
Distributed in the United States by North-South Books Inc., New York 10016.
Library of Congress Cataloging-in-Publication Data is available.
Printed in China by Leo Paper Products Ltd., Heshan, Guangdong, June 2012.
ISBN: 978-0-7358-4092-8
1 3 5 7 9 • 10 8 6 4 2

www.northsouth.com

HEINZ JANISCH

Why is the Snow White?

WITH ILLUSTRATIONS BY

SILKE LEFFLER

TRANSLATED BY REBECCA K. MORRISON

NorthSouth
New York / London

It was snowing outside. Mira was wearing her white pajamas and skipping around the room.

"Tell me a fairytale," she said to her father. "A window fairytale."

They fetched a cozy blanket and settled down on the windowsill. They gazed out at the swirling snowflakes for a while. Mira's father pointed to the white rooftops.

"Do you know why the snow is white?"

Mira shook her head. She snuggled down and drew her toes in beneath the blanket. . . .

Once, a long, long time ago, the snow was as colorless and transparent as the wind. Until one day Father Snow came upon a meadow full of bright flowers. He was astonished. Such an array of beautiful colors! He asked the violet whether she might grant him some of her purple color.

"Why, yes! How pretty that would look!" said the violet. The snow began to shimmer a wonderful purple.

"But I . . . *I* need my color," the violet cried hastily, snatching back her purple hue.

On Father Snow went. He asked the sunflower whether he might have a little of her yellow.

"Why, yes! How pretty that would look!" said the sunflower.

The snow began to gleam a sunflower-yellow.

"But I . . . I need my color," the sunflower cried suddenly, snatching back her yellow gleam.

On Father Snow went. He asked
the red rose whether he might have a
little of her red.

"Why, yes! How pretty that would
look!" exclaimed the rose.

And soon the snow was draped
in glowing red.

"But I . . . *I* need my color," cried
the rose impetuously, snatching back
her red radiance.

On Father Snow went. He asked a slender blade of grass whether he might have a little of his green.

"Why, yes! How pretty that would look!" said the blade of grass. The snow was promptly decked in green.

"But I . . . *I* need my color," the blade of grass cried bitterly, snatching back his green glow.

On Father Snow went. He asked the blue
cornflower whether he might have a little
of her blue.

"Why, yes! How pretty that would look!"
the cornflower said. The snow soon glittered
blue in the sunlight.

"But I . . . *I* need my color," the cornflower
cried carelessly, snatching back her color blue.

Father Snow asked the striped leaf.
And the pink blossom. He asked
the brightly spotted and the
patchwork flowers. But not one
was willing to part with a little
of their color.

Just when Father Snow was about to give up, he noticed a small white flower with tiny bells.

Plucking up his courage, he posed his question one last time.

"Why, yes!" the small flower said. "If you like my color, then you are welcome to have some."

And that is why the snow is white. Marvelously, radiantly white.

Ever since he has proudly displayed his white mantle, on every street and every rooftop, on every meadow and every field.

As for those flowers and leaves and blades of grass, well, he still does not look on them kindly. He buries them beneath his whiteness whenever he can. The only flower he never touches is the small white flower with her tiny bells. In the winter she stands out clearly.

Intro

The small white flower came to be known as
the snowdrop—she had shared her beautiful white
color with the snow, after all.

Mira watched the white snowflakes sailing
through the sky past her window.
"Did you make that up?" she asked her father.
He shook his head.
"It is an old fairytale. I just embroidered it a little."
Mira nodded.
"Tomorrow I will tell you why the snow is white,"
she said.
She gave him a kiss and clambered down from
the windowsill.
Then, with a hop and a jump, she landed on
the soft, warm bed.